TATE MCGHEE

Legends of Paradise Key

Contents

1   The Vanishing Paradise: Luke witnesses
the rapid...   1

2   Tale that Ignited our Journey   8

3   Taking Charge: Luke rallies his friends to
save Paradise Key...   12

4   Lost in the Depths   16

5   The Enigmatic Manor: Unveiling Secrets   20

6   Torn Between Love and Loyalty   24

7   Past Lives and Mystical Tales   28

8   Temptation's Test: Luke faces a moral
dilemma that threatens...   32

9   Artistic Discoveries   34

10   Ghostly Encounters: Lessons in Courage   36

11   The Necklace's Countdown: Friends'
Race Against Demolition   40

12   Trapped in Pursuit   44

13   Redemption's Path   48

14   United We Stand   53

15   A Mysterious Guide   57

16   The Necklace's Hidden Potential   61

17   Battle for Paradise Key   65

18   Community United: Rallying for Preservation   71

19   The Legacy of Heroes   74

About the Author   78

Also by Tate McGhee 81

1

The Vanishing Paradise: Luke witnesses the rapid transformation of his neighborhood, igniting a sense of urgency to protect Paradise Key.

Luke woke to the jarring sound of heavy machinery echoing through his bedroom window. The grating noise pierced his peaceful morning routine, shattering the tranquility he had come to cherish. He sat up in bed, rubbing his eyes and trying to shake off the grogginess, but the reality of the destruction unfolding outside became impossible to ignore.

Drawing open his curtains, Luke was greeted by a sight that sent a wave of sadness crashing over him. The once-grand building that stood just across the street from his house was now being torn down, its walls succumbing to the relentless assault of bulldozers and wrecking balls. Dust clouds billowed into the air as chunks of debris crashed to the ground, erasing decades of memories.

As Luke stared at the chaos before him, a profound sense of loss washed over him. It wasn't merely the demolition of bricks and mortar; it was the erasure of history, a piece of his own heritage vanishing right before his eyes. He couldn't help but feel an ache deep within his chest, as if a vital part of his community was being torn away.

Determined to confront the developers responsible for this senseless destruction, Luke stepped outside onto his porch. The air was thick with the scent of dust and cement, a harsh reminder of the changing landscape he now found himself in. With each step he took towards the construction site, anger burned within him, fueled by an overwhelming desire to fight for what remained of Paradise Key.

As Luke approached the chaos, a small group of protesters caught his attention. Their signs were emblazoned with messages that mirrored his own outrage: "Preserve Our Heritage!" and "Save Paradise Key!" They chanted slogans that resonated deep within Luke's soul, their shared determination emboldening him further.

A knot formed in Luke's stomach as he faced the developers responsible for obliterating his neighborhood's identity. They stood near the wrecking ball, engrossed in their plans for yet another faceless, cookie-cutter structure. Their arrogance radiated off them like a toxic aura, leaving Luke struck by a mix of anger and vulnerability.

Taking a deep breath, Luke steadied himself and approached one of the developers. The man towered over him, his cold stare betraying a sense of entitlement that made Luke's blood boil. But he couldn't back down now; he had to make them see reason.

With shaky hands and a voice laced with urgency, Luke poured his heart out. He painted a vivid picture of Paradise Key's rich history and cultural significance, emphasizing the importance of preserving its charm and character. Every word he spoke was fueled by love for his community, by the memories that were being crushed under the weight of progress.

But the developer scoffed at Luke's heartfelt plea, dismissing him as inconsequential in the face of progress and economic growth. His condescending words hung heavy in the air, shattering Luke's hope that reason might prevail. The frustration bubbled within him, threatening to overflow, but he knew that reasoning with these developers would be futile.

With a heavy heart but a mind brimming with determination, Luke walked away from the construction site. He left behind the developers and their empty promises, their hollow dreams of luxury condos and shopping centers. As he retraced his steps towards home, his mind spun with ideas on how to save Paradise Key. And little did he know that this encounter was merely the beginning of a thrilling adventure that would test his resolve and bring him closer to unraveling a century-old legend.

Luke knew he couldn't do it alone. Gathering his close-knit group of friends at a local café seemed like the next logical step. With worry etched on their faces, they listened intently as Luke shared his concerns about the future of their community. The faded photographs adorning the café's walls served as a reminder of happier times in Paradise Key, a stark contrast to the turmoil unfolding outside.

One by one, his friends entered the café, their faces reflecting a mix of curiosity and concern. Pete slid into the seat across from Luke, wearing an expression of curiosity tinged with concern. Nate and Violet joined them, their presence offering a comforting sense of solidarity. Madison entered soon after, her eyes wide with anticipation, ready to lend her support. They all settled in, the aroma of freshly brewed coffee filling the air, grounding them in this pivotal moment.

Taking a steadying breath, Luke began his tale of destruction, recounting the heartbreaking scene he had witnessed that morning. The group listened intently, their expressions shifting from surprise to anger as Luke's words resonated with each of them. The gravity of the situation weighed heavily on each of them, as they realized that their beloved Paradise Key was under threat.

Exchanging worried glances and nodding in agreement, the friends formed an unspoken pact. A collective determination rose within them—a shared understanding that they must take action to protect their community, to fight for its heritage. As they left the café that day, hope surged within their hearts, propelling them forward into the unknown. Together, they would embark on a gripping adventure that would test their friendship and ultimately lead them to discover the power of legends.

Luke entered the small café, its warm and inviting atmosphere offering solace amidst the chaos unfolding outside. The familiar scent of freshly brewed coffee filled the air, instantly calming his racing thoughts. He knew that gathering his close-knit group of friends here was the next logical step in their quest to save Paradise Key.

One by one, Luke's closest friends filtered into the café, their faces a mix of curiosity and concern. Pete slid into the seat across from Luke, a questioning look in his eyes. Nate and Violet took their spots beside them, their expressions mirroring the worry etched on Luke's face. Madison joined in soon after, her eyes wide with anticipation.

As they settled around the table, Luke took a deep breath and began sharing his worries. The words flowed freely from his lips, painting a vivid image of the destruction he had witnessed earlier that morning. The faded photographs adorning the café's walls served as a poignant backdrop, showcasing happier times in Paradise Key - a stark contrast to the turmoil unfolding outside.

His friends listened intently, their eyes fixed on Luke's every word. Pete's furrowed brow mirrored his concern for their community. Nate's jaw clenched as he absorbed the magnitude of what was happening. Violet's fingers tapped nervously against her coffee cup, her mind racing with possibilities. And Madison's gaze never wavered from Luke's face, her unwavering support evident in her unwavering presence.

As Luke finished speaking, a heavy silence hung in the air. Each friend exchanged worried glances, their expressions shifting from surprise to anger as they fully grasped the gravity of the situation facing their beloved Paradise Key. They understood that this wasn't just about preserving buildings and structures; it was about safeguarding a heritage that was deeply ingrained in their souls.

Pete broke the silence, his voice filled with determination and resolve. "We can't stand by and let them destroy everything we hold dear," he declared, his eyes meeting each of his friends'. "We have to find a way to fight back."

Nods of agreement rippled through the group, a shared understanding passing between them. As they gazed at one another, their eyes alight with a renewed sense of purpose, a sense of unity enveloped the café. They knew that time was running out, that they had to act swiftly and decisively to protect their community.

Luke reached out, his hand finding Pete's across the table. Their fingers intertwined in a powerful gesture of solidarity and friendship. "We'll do whatever it takes," Luke affirmed, his voice filled with conviction. "Together, we can save our home."

The others echoed his sentiment, their voices rising in unison, as if they were casting a spell of determination upon themselves. They were bound by a common love for Paradise Key and fueled by their shared anger at its impending destruction. With every word spoken, their collective resolve grew stronger.

And so, as they left the café that day, hope burned brightly in their hearts. Their adventure had just begun, and little did they know the challenges and obstacles awaiting them. But armed with friendship and the power of legends, they were ready to face whatever lay ahead - to navigate treacherous swamps and crumbling mansions, to outsmart greedy developers, and to unravel the secrets of a century-old legend.

Together, they would change the course of their community's destiny. They would defy the odds and preserve Paradise Key's heritage. And in doing so, they would discover the true power of legends - not just in stories passed down through generations, but in the strength and determination of a group of close-knit friends who refused to let their home be erased from history.

2

Tale that Ignited our Journey

The warm glow of candlelight bathed Nate's living room as the group settled onto their plush bean bags, their eyes fixed on him. The enticing aroma of freshly baked cookies filled the air, adding to the cozy atmosphere. It was a perfect summer evening, and they were ready to delve into the mysterious legend that had captured their imaginations.

Luke sat with a proud yet protective demeanor, keeping a watchful eye on his younger sister, Madison. Pete fidgeted eagerly on his bean bag, unable to contain his excitement for what lay ahead. Nate leaned forward, his eyes shining with a mixture of creativity and wonder. Violet wriggled with anticipation beside Pete, her curiosity evident in her every move. Madison rested quietly, her bright eyes reflecting her eagerness to contribute.

As Nate gently unfolded the aged map before them, its crinkling sound seemed to release a sense of anticipation, as if they were about to unveil long-hidden secrets. The parchment texture added an air of mystique to their gathering, entwining their senses with the rich history of Paradise Key. Their gaze was drawn to faded ink lines that depicted their coastal community and its surrounding areas—an intricate web of paths waiting to be explored. The map held the promise of adventure and untold treasures.

With bated breath, the group traced their fingers along the lines on the map, their minds transported to a time when legends were born. As Nate's voice took on an almost storytelling cadence, their attention was fully captured. The warm glow of the candlelight danced across the walls, casting flickering shadows that seemed to whisper secrets known only to the map.

Nate wove together bits of historical facts and imaginative fabrications, creating a tapestry of myth and wonder. His words called forth images of the lost diamond necklace and its rumored powers—a jewel that could grant wishes, reveal hidden truths, and offer protection from harm. Excitement sparkled in the eyes of each friend, their imaginations ignited by the possibilities that lay before them.

Violet interjected with her findings about curses and ancient ghosts haunting Paradise Key, her voice filled with a blend of trepidation and fascination. She shared tales of restless spirits wandering through the decaying mansions, and whispered accounts of ghostly footsteps echoing through long-forgotten hallways. A shiver ran down their spines as they contemplated the unknown realms that existed within their beloved neighborhood.

Pete's eyes gleamed with enthusiasm as he envisioned the adventure ahead. His energy was contagious, reigniting a sense of excitement in the room. He proposed following clues left by previous treasure hunters who had attempted but failed to locate the necklace. The group nodded in agreement, their minds racing with thoughts of hidden maps, clever riddles, and uncharted territories waiting to be explored.

Luke listened intently, his brow furrowed as he considered the weight of their undertaking. He felt a profound responsibility for his community, knowing that finding the lost necklace could empower them in their fight against the encroaching destruction. Determination burned in his eyes as he silently vowed to do whatever it took to protect Paradise Key.

Nate's eyes sparkled with a contagious sense of adventure as he added his artistic vision to the mix. He suggested they start their exploration by investigating the abandoned mansions scattered throughout Paradise Key—those forgotten relics that held untold secrets within their crumbling walls. Their hearts raced at the thought of unlocking the mysteries that lay beneath layers of dust and decay.

With curiosity piqued and excitement filling the room, the group settled deeper into their bean bags. They exchanged knowing glances—an unspoken understanding passing between them. They were ready to embark on a thrilling adventure, armed with friendship, the power of legends, and an unwavering belief in their ability to make a difference.

Little did they know that this gathering would mark the beginning of a journey that would test their resolve, challenge their perceptions, and bring them face-to-face with untold wonders and unimaginable dangers. But together, they were ready to face whatever lay ahead and prove that the power of legends could change the course of their community's destiny.

3

Taking Charge: Luke rallies his friends to save Paradise Key as danger looms.

As the sun began to set over Paradise Key, Luke and his friends gathered on the golden sands of the beach. The salty breeze rustled through their hair, carrying with it a sense of anticipation and purpose. The warm glow of the setting sun bathed them in a soft golden light, as if nature itself was lending its support to their cause.

Luke took a deep breath, feeling a surge of energy coursing through his veins. He looked around at his friends, their faces filled with determination. Pete's eyes gleamed with excitement, his boundless enthusiasm infectious. Violet's fiery red hair caught the last rays of sunlight, her passion for justice shining through. Madison, always wise beyond her years, gazed up at Luke with unwavering trust and belief. They were a team, united by a common goal—to save their beloved community.

"Tonight," Luke declared, his voice steady yet full of conviction, "we take the first step in reclaiming our community."

Pete pumped his fist in the air, unable to contain his excitement. "Yeah! Let's show them what we're made of!"

Violet nodded fervently, her vibrant green eyes flashing with determination. "We won't let them destroy everything we hold dear. It's time to fight back."

Madison squeezed Luke's hand tightly, her small fingers offering a reassuring presence. "I believe in you, big brother. We'll make a difference together."

Luke smiled at his sister's unwavering faith and squeezed her hand back. Then he turned to face the crowd that had gathered before them—a sea of concerned faces filled with hope and apprehension.

Stepping onto the makeshift stage that had been set up near the center of the gathering, Luke felt a surge of adrenaline. This was the moment they had been working towards—the moment when they would expose the truth and ignite the flame of resistance within their community.

"Good evening, fellow residents of Paradise Key," Luke began, his voice strong and steady. "We stand before you today not just as friends, but as individuals who deeply love this community we call home. We have uncovered evidence of corruption and deceit within the very fabric of our neighborhood."

A murmur rippled through the crowd, a mix of curiosity and concern. All eyes were fixed on Luke, waiting to hear what he had to say.

Luke continued, his voice growing more powerful with each word. "Developers may have power and money, but they cannot extinguish our passion and love for this place. We have come together to fight against their plans for profit at the expense of our heritage."

Pete stepped forward, his voice carrying a mix of anger and determination. "We won't let them take away what makes Paradise Key unique—the swaying palm trees, the endless stretch of beach, the sense of community that binds us together."

Violet added her passionate voice to the mix, her words ringing with conviction. "We have evidence that exposes their true intentions, their web of deceit. Together, we can shine a light on their dark dealings and protect what is rightfully ours."

The crowd erupted into applause, their voices united in support of Luke and his friends. It was a stirring moment—a moment that marked the beginning of a united front against the forces threatening to destroy Paradise Key.

As the applause subsided, Luke's eyes scanned the sea of faces before him. In that moment, he saw not just individuals, but a community bound by history and shared experiences. He felt a surge of pride knowing that they were not alone in this fight.

"With your help," Luke declared, his voice carrying across the gathering, "we can reclaim our community. Together, we can make a difference. Let us stand as one against those who seek to erase our history."

The crowd roared with approval, their voices echoing through the night. Luke and his friends exchanged proud smiles, knowing that the fight had only just begun. They were no longer simply a group of friends—they were leaders, activists, and guardians of Paradise Key.

As the crowd dispersed, with renewed determination burning in their hearts, Luke turned to his friends. "We've made our mark tonight," he said, his voice filled with a sense of purpose. "But there is much more work to be done. Let's keep pushing forward, together."

And so, as the night sky enveloped Paradise Key, Luke and his friends walked into the unknown future. Armed with evidence, passion, and the unwavering support of their community, they would face whatever challenges lay ahead. The battle for Paradise Key had begun, and they were determined to win it.

4

Lost in the Depths

Luke's concerns lingered in the back of his mind as he stood on the edge of the treacherous swamps. The dense foliage seemed to swallow up the sunlight, creating an eerie atmosphere that sent a shiver down his spine. As he glanced at his friends, he could tell they shared his sense of unease.

Pete, always the adventurous one, bounded forward, undeterred by their surroundings. "Come on, guys!" he called out with unwavering enthusiasm. "The swamps hold the key to saving Paradise Key. We can't let fear hold us back!"

Violet, her fiery red hair catching the faint light that seeped through the trees, stepped closer to Luke. "Luke, I understand your concerns," she said softly. "But think about what's at stake. Our community is on the brink of destruction. We have to be willing to face these unknown dangers for the greater good."

Luke nodded reluctantly, his worries simmering just beneath the surface. He knew that their mission was crucial, but he couldn't help but fear for the safety of his friends. He clenched his fists, trying to summon the courage within him.

As they ventured deeper into the swamps, Nate took the lead. His knowledge of local wildlife and survival skills instilled a sense of confidence in the group. They watched as he navigated through the murky waters and avoided potential hazards.

Suddenly, they came across a gator-infested pool that blocked their path. Pete's eyes widened with excitement as he took a step closer, itching to explore. But Luke's protective instincts kicked in.

"Pete, wait!" Luke called out urgently, reaching out to stop him. "We need to be cautious. These waters are swarming with alligators."

Pete hesitated for a moment before grinning mischievously. "Don't worry, Luke," he reassured with a wink. "I've got this."

Before Luke could protest further, Pete grabbed a sturdy branch and began pounding it against the ground, creating vibrations that mimicked the sound of a larger predator. The alligators, startled by the presence of potential competition, scattered into the depths of the swamp.

The group let out a collective sigh of relief as Pete tossed the branch aside, his face beaming with triumph. Luke couldn't help but shake his head, a mixture of annoyance and gratitude filling his chest.

"You're lucky that worked," Luke muttered, unable to hide a small smile.

Pete clapped him on the back, his spirit undeterred. "You worry too much, my friend," he said with a laugh. "We've got each other's backs. We're in this together."

As they continued their journey through the treacherous swamps, they stumbled upon hidden symbols carved into trees and rocks. The intricate designs sparked their curiosity, and they couldn't help but feel that they were inching closer to a breakthrough.

Luke knelt down beside one particularly elaborate symbol, tracing its ancient lines with his fingertips. "These symbols hold the key to unraveling the mysteries of Paradise Key," he mused, his voice filled with determination. "We're on the right path."

His friends gathered around him, their eyes filled with anticipation. They knew that this adventure was about more than just saving their community—it was about preserving their heritage and defying the forces that threatened to erase them from existence.

Together, they pressed forward, their steps purposeful and resolute. As they delved deeper into the heart of the swamps, they carried with them a sense of unity and hope. They may have been surrounded by danger and uncertainty, but Luke and his friends were determined to confront whatever challenges lay ahead.

With every step they took, they grew closer to unraveling the secrets of Paradise Key. The legends whispered through the rustling leaves and echoed in their hearts, guiding them towards a path that would lead to victory.

As the sun dipped below the horizon, casting a warm golden glow across the swamp, Luke's concerns began to fade away. The determination in his friends' eyes ignited a fire within him, pushing him forward on this perilous journey.

Paradise Key may be under siege, but with each passing moment, they grew stronger. They were no longer just a group of friends—they were a force to be reckoned with. And as they ventured deeper into the swamps, they knew that their fight was only just beginning.

5

The Enigmatic Manor: Unveiling Secrets

The group cautiously entered the abandoned mansion, their flashlights illuminating the dusty hallways. Luke, Violet, Pete, Nate, and Madison split up to search for any signs of hidden passages or clues about the mystical necklace. The air was thick with anticipation as they ventured deeper into the dimly lit rooms, their footsteps echoing off the decaying walls.

Luke's heart pounded in his chest as he entered the vast dining hall of the abandoned mansion. The once grand space was now reduced to faded wallpaper and crumbling furniture. His flashlight beam danced across the intricate wood carvings on the table, desperately searching for any sign of a hidden compartment or secret message.

Violet carefully made her way up the creaky staircase, her gaze fixated on an ornate chandelier hanging precariously above. Dust particles floated in the beam of her flashlight, casting an ethereal glow on the worn carpet beneath her feet. She couldn't help but feel a sense of awe and reverence for the history contained within these walls.

Meanwhile, Pete bounded up another flight of stairs, leading to what appeared to be a study. His excitement grew with every step he took, his eyes scanning the shelves filled with tattered books and weathered maps. He hoped to find any indication of hidden compartments or secret passageways that might lead them closer to the truth about the mystical necklace.

Nate examined every inch of a grand ballroom, his keen eye for detail taking in the faded wallpaper and intricate patterns etched into the walls. His fingers traced the ornate designs, hoping to discover a hidden clue or whisper from the past. The room seemed frozen in time, preserving an aura of opulence and grandeur that captivated his imagination.

Down a dimly lit hallway lined with portraits, Madison tiptoed quietly. Her young eyes widened with curiosity as she studied each face, searching for any hint of clues hidden within the faded brushstrokes. She felt a connection to these long-forgotten figures; their sorrowful gazes seemed to carry untold stories, waiting to be discovered.

As they explored different rooms and stumbled upon forgotten corners of the mansion, their excitement grew. Each discovery intensified their determination to unravel the mysteries that lay hidden within its walls. Torn photographs hinted at bygone eras, their faded faces capturing their imaginations and fueling their resolve.

Finally, the friends regrouped in the grand foyer, their faces illuminated by excitement and intrigue. They shared their findings, each revelation urging them forward on their quest for the truth about Paradise Key.

"The history within these walls is tangible," Violet said, her voice filled with awe. "It's like we've stepped back in time."

Nate nodded in agreement, his eyes shining with reverence. "Imagine the stories these walls could tell if they could speak."

Luke stared at the intricate wood carvings on the dining table, his mind racing with possibilities. "There must be hidden compartments or secret passages," he said determinedly. "We have to keep searching."

Pete's enthusiasm overflowed as he waved a tattered map triumphantly. "Look what I found!" he exclaimed. "This map could lead us to hidden treasures or secret tunnels!"

Madison clutched her favorite torn photograph, her young voice filled with wonder. "Do you think these people knew about the necklace?" she asked, her eyes wide with innocence. "Maybe they left clues behind."

As they stood together in the grand foyer, a renewed sense of purpose filled the air. Each piece of evidence they had uncovered fueled their determination to uncover the secrets that lay hidden within the decaying mansion.

"We're onto something big," Luke declared with conviction. "The legends whispered through these corridors—they want us to push forward, to uncover the truth that has long been obscured."

Their quest for the hidden passages and clues about the mystical necklace had only just begun. Yet, with each step they took, their bond grew stronger, and their resolve to protect Paradise Key and unveil its secrets deepened.

Together, they stood ready to face whatever mysteries lay ahead. The legends had chosen them for a reason, and the power of their friendship would guide them through the darkness.

The abandoned mansion held secrets begging to be revealed. And as they stepped forward with renewed purpose, a sense of exhilaration mingled with trepidation, for they were on the verge of uncovering the mysteries that would ultimately save Paradise Key.

Excitement filled their hearts as they embarked on the next phase of their adventure—one step closer to unraveling the secrets that had been concealed within these decaying walls.

6

Torn Between Love and Loyalty

Pete's heart raced as he watched his sister, Madison, confidently navigate a treacherous obstacle. She had always been brave and determined, but in that moment, Pete couldn't help but feel both proud of her resilience and anxious about the dangers she could face.

His protective instincts clashed with his yearning to be by his friends' side, creating a swirling storm of conflicting emotions within him. The group had become like family to Pete, especially Luke, who had been his closest friend since they were children. But Madison was his blood, his little sister, and he felt an overwhelming responsibility to keep her safe.

As they regrouped after successfully overcoming the obstacle, Pete found himself drawn to Luke's steady presence. He needed someone to confide in, someone who understood the weight of his dilemma.

Sitting on a fallen log near the edge of the swamp, Pete poured out his fears and desires. Luke listened attentively, nodding sympathetically as Pete spoke. He understood the struggle that Pete faced, torn between loyalty to their mission and the need to protect his sister.

"Look, Pete," Luke began gently, placing a comforting hand on Pete's shoulder. "I know it's hard. We all care about Madison. But we can't let fear dictate our decisions. Our mission is not just about one person—it's about preserving our community and heritage as a whole."

Pete nodded, understanding the gravity of their fight against the developers who threatened to destroy Paradise Key. "I know you're right, Luke," he said softly. "But sometimes it feels like I'm being pulled in two different directions. I don't want to let down my friends or betray Madison's trust."

Luke squeezed Pete's shoulder reassuringly. "We're all here for you, Pete. We understand the conflict you're facing. But together, we can navigate these challenges. We'll find a way to keep Madison safe and continue our quest. We're stronger together."

Pete took a deep breath, his mind racing with the potential consequences of each decision. Could he truly protect his sister while still staying true to his friends? The weight of these choices hung heavy on his shoulders, knowing that any path he chose would have lasting implications for all involved.

The group began to make their way through the thick un-derbrush, relying on their instincts and the clues they had uncovered. As they moved forward, Pete's internal struggle deepened, but he also began to realize the strength of their bond.

In the heat of their search, danger suddenly struck. They found themselves faced with a perilous obstacle that put Madison directly in harm's way. Pete's heart lurched in his chest as he saw his sister's safety compromised. Without a second thought, he leaped into action, pushing himself beyond his limits to save her.

His protective instincts kicked into high gear as adrenaline coursed through his veins. He disregarded his own safety, focused solely on rescuing Madison from the imminent danger that lurked nearby. In that moment, Pete's actions revealed the intensity of the conflict within him—the fierce loyalty he felt towards both his sister and his friends.

As he pulled Madison to safety, her small frame trembling in his arms, a wave of relief washed over Pete. They had narrowly escaped catastrophe thanks to their quick thinking and resourcefulness. But the experience also served as a catalyst for Pete's resolve to navigate the conflicts that lay ahead.

As the dust settled and they caught their breath, Pete looked around at his friends—his chosen family. In their eyes, he saw understanding and acceptance. They had all faced their own struggles and doubts, but they remained united in their mission to protect Paradise Key.

Their journey was far from over, and Pete knew that more challenges awaited them. But with every step they took, their collective bond grew stronger. Pete couldn't ignore the fact that his friends' skills and cooperation were crucial for their survival. He was beginning to understand that protecting Madison meant embracing their unity.

Together, they stood ready to face whatever mysteries lay ahead. The legends had chosen them for a reason, and the power of their friendship would guide them through the darkness. Pete's conflicted loyalty began to resolve as he acknowledged the strength of their collective bond and the importance of embracing their unity in the face of adversity.

As they continued their quest, Pete knew that he would always prioritize his sister's safety, but he also understood that he didn't have to choose between his family and his friends. They were one and the same—a tight-knit group with a shared purpose.

Pete's dilemma had awakened a deeper understanding within him—the realization that they were stronger together, and that by protecting Madison, he was also protecting everything they fought for. With each step they took, their resolve grew stronger, and Pete felt a newfound sense of peace within himself.

Their adventure had only just begun, and Pete was ready to face whatever challenges lay ahead. Conflicting loyalties no longer weighed him down; instead, they fueled his determination to protect his sister and preserve the magic of Paradise Key.

7

Past Lives and Mystical Tales

The library was filled with the hushed rustling of pages and the occasional squeak of chairs as the group delved into their respective sections. Luke's eyes scanned the shelves, searching for any historical texts that might shed light on the diamond necklace's past. He could feel a buzz of excitement building within him, knowing that the answers they sought could be hidden within these dusty tomes.

Violet diligently pored over books in the history section, her fingers gently turning each page as she absorbed every detail. She was captivated by the stories of Paradise Key's early settlers and their connection to the necklace. The weight of history settled upon her shoulders, fueling her determination to unravel the mysteries that lay ahead.

Nate, his brows furrowed in concentration, immersed himself in ancient mythology and folklore. He knew that legends often held kernels of truth, and he hoped to discover clues that would guide them through their journey. His mind danced with images of mythical creatures and heroes as he attempted to connect their tales to the necklace's mystical powers.

Meanwhile, Pete and Madison combed through stacks of newspapers, searching for any mentions of the necklace or its previous owners. The old pages crinkled beneath their touch as they meticulously scanned columns and headlines. Pete's heart raced with each promising lead they uncovered, eager to piece together the puzzle that had brought them all together.

Luke's gaze fell upon an aging manuscript in the special collections section of the library. Its delicate pages whispered secrets as his fingers delicately turned them, revealing forgotten stories of Paradise Key's past. He read about lost treasures, curses, and ancient rituals—each word driving his curiosity further.

Hours passed in a blur as they delved deeper into their research. Snippets of information were pieced together like a mosaic painting, revealing fragments of the necklace's story. Names and dates became threads that wove together the tapestry of Paradise Key's history. The weight of their discovery settled upon their shoulders, filling them with a renewed sense of purpose.

With notebooks filled with scribbled notes and minds overflowing with newfound knowledge, they reconvened at a small table in the library. Their eyes met, each reflecting a shared dedication to their mission. The air crackled with anticipation as they prepared to share their findings.

Luke spoke first, his voice steadying the room. "I've discovered tales of an ancient civilization that once thrived in this area," he said. "They believed the necklace held immense power—a key to preserving their home amidst countless challenges."

"Indeed," Violet chimed in, her voice filled with excitement. "And I found records of our own ancestors wearing the necklace in old photographs! It seems it has been a part of our family's history for generations."

Nate nodded, eager to contribute to the discussion. "Mythology and folklore suggest that those who possessed the necklace were bestowed with extraordinary abilities—gifts that helped them protect Paradise Key in times of peril."

Pete and Madison exchanged glances, brimming with anticipation as they revealed their discoveries. "We unearthed articles detailing a series of thefts throughout history," Pete explained. "Each time the necklace disappeared, chaos ensued. There are legends of lost treasures and hidden curses tied to its disappearance."

The room fell silent as they absorbed the weight of their findings. The diamond necklace held not only historical significance but also mystical powers capable of preserving Paradise Key's magic.

"We've come a long way," Luke said, breaking the silence. "But there is still much more to discover. We must follow every lead, uncover every clue to protect our community and preserve its heritage."

Agreement shone in their eyes as they closed their notebooks and rose from the table. With renewed determination radiating from within, they knew they had taken an important step forward. The library had served as a gateway to the necklace's history, lighting the path toward their shared destiny.

As they exited the library, a sense of awe washed over them. The sun cast long shadows across the landscape, and an ocean breeze carried whispers of legends yet to be told. They were ready to embark on the next phase of their journey—guided by the centuries-old stories that bound them together, they would uncover the true power of the diamond necklace and save Paradise Key from destruction.

8

Temptation's Test: Luke faces a moral dilemma that threatens to shake his loyalty to his friends.

Nate sat alone in his cluttered room, surrounded by crumpled sketches and unfinished paintings. The flickering light of a desk lamp illuminated his face, casting shadows that mirrored the turmoil within him. His brows furrowed as he stared at each piece, his fingers tracing the delicate lines, but his confidence wavered.

Self-doubt seeped into Nate's thoughts like a creeping fog, obscuring the vibrant colors of his creativity. He questioned whether his artistic talent was truly enough to make a difference in their mission or if it was merely an insignificant brushstroke in the grand tapestry of life. Memories of past criticisms from his parents and friends resurfaced, their words echoing in his mind like a haunting refrain.

His gaze wandered to the corner of his room where a dusty easel stood, adorned with a canvas covered in half-formed ideas. It seemed to taunt him, a reminder of his perceived inadequacy. The weight of their expectations pressed down on his shoulders, threatening to smother his creative spark.

But amidst the doubts that threatened to consume him, a flicker of determination ignited. Nate's face reflected a mixture of frustration, fear, and hope as he wrestled with these conflicting emotions. He knew deep down that art had the power to move hearts and minds, even if it seemed small in the grand scheme of things.

In search of solace and inspiration, Nate decided to take a break from the confines of his room. He ventured outside into the fading daylight and found himself drawn to the nearby coastal path. The salty breeze caressed his face, carrying with it whispers of legends and untold stories.

9

Artistic Discoveries

As Nate walked along the path, he noticed a small rock painted with intricate patterns nestled amidst the wildflowers. Curiosity piqued, Nate picked it up and turned it over in his hands. The delicate strokes and vibrant colors on the rock mesmerized him, reminding him of the power of art to bring beauty into the world.

Nate's steps quickened, his heart pounding with newfound determination. He knew that he needed to find a way to break free from the shackles of self-doubt and embrace his artistic talents fully. They couldn't afford to let doubt hinder their mission to preserve Paradise Key.

With renewed purpose, Nate returned to his room and faced the easel, his hand reluctantly picking up a paintbrush. He didn't know what would emerge from the depths of his creativity, but he was ready to unleash it onto the canvas.

Hours turned into moments as Nate lost himself in the act of creation. The world around him faded into the background as vibrant hues and unexpected textures emerged beneath his fingertips. Doubt melted away with each stroke, replaced by a blossoming confidence in his artistic abilities.

As he stepped back to admire the painting, a sense of pride welled up within him. This artwork carried a piece of his soul, an expression of his unique perspective. It was imperfect, just like he was, but it held the potential to touch others' lives.

In that moment, Nate realized that his artistic journey wasn't about perfection or conforming to others' expectations; it was about embracing his true self and adding his voice to the world. With every stroke of his brush, he would paint a path toward saving Paradise Key, infusing it with the magic of legends and the power of art.

10

Ghostly Encounters: Lessons in Courage

Violet's insatiable curiosity got the best of her as the group was engrossed in deciphering clues. While Luke, Nate, Pete, and Madison were deeply involved in their research at the library, Violet's eyes wandered to a peculiar trail of faded footprints leading deeper into an abandoned mansion. The old house stood before her like a forgotten relic, its weathered facade quietly beckoning her to explore its secrets.

Unable to resist the mysterious pull, Violet excused herself from the table, whispering promises to return soon. She couldn't shake the feeling that the answers they sought were hidden within the walls of this decaying mansion. The thrill of adventure coursed through her veins as she embarked on her solo expedition.

With each step she took, the weight of anticipation settled upon her shoulders. The mansion's dark hallways stretched out before Violet like an intricate maze, each turn revealing more secrets hidden within its decaying walls. Shadows danced and flickered, playing tricks on her eyes. A gentle breeze whispered through cracks in the windows, carrying with it the echoes of legends long passed.

As Violet ventured deeper into the heart of the mansion, she could feel a sense of foreboding settle upon her. The air grew heavy with an otherworldly presence, sending shivers down her spine. But her determination pushed her forward, for she knew that uncovering the mysteries hidden within these halls was essential to their mission.

After what felt like hours of exploration, Violet stumbled upon a hidden room tucked away in a forgotten corner of the mansion. It seemed frozen in time, filled with artifacts that whispered stories of days gone by. Old photographs lined the walls, their faded images capturing moments of joy and struggle. She reached out to touch one photograph depicting a bygone era when suddenly, a chill ran down her spine.

In the dim light of the room, a figure materialized before Violet. It appeared translucent and ethereal, its presence radiating with an otherworldly aura. The ghostly figure's eyes met hers, conveying a mix of sadness and hope. Trembling, Violet found herself unable to look away.

Silence settled between them, broken only by the quiet hum of the wind. The ghostly figure beckoned Violet closer, its voice a mere whisper in her ear. It spoke of the struggles faced by previous generations, the hardships endured in the face of adversity. Through each tale of resilience and bravery, Violet learned that courage was not the absence of fear, but rather the strength to push through despite it.

As she listened intently to the ghostly figure's stories, Violet felt a deep connection to the history of Paradise Key itself. The sacrifices made by those who came before her echoed in her heart, fueling her determination to fight for her community and the preservation of their heritage. She understood that she had been chosen to carry on the legacy of those who had gone before.

With a sense of gratitude and purpose, Violet bid farewell to the ghostly figure, feeling an inner strength and conviction that she had never felt before. As she retraced her steps through the labyrinthine hallways of the mansion, her heart raced with a mix of anticipation and relief. Emerging from the shadows into the waiting arms of her friends, she knew that she had undergone a profound transformation.

Breathless and wide-eyed, Violet shared her encounter with the ghostly figure. Her words were filled with wonder and awe as she recounted the lessons she had learned. The group gathered around her, their eyes reflecting both curiosity and deep respect for the significance of her experience.

Inspired by Violet's encounter and newfound bravery, they recognized the importance of their friendship and the strength that lay within their unity. With renewed determination, they pressed forward, knowing that their bond and shared purpose would guide them through whatever challenges lay ahead. United in their mission, they set out to find the lost diamond necklace and save Paradise Key from the impending destruction.

A new chapter had begun, one where legends and reality intertwined, where courage would be tested, and the power of friendship and heritage would light the way.

11

The Necklace's Countdown: Friends' Race Against Demolition

Nate's heart raced as he followed his friends through the dense mangroves. The swamp was alive with the symphony of chirping insects and croaking frogs, their melodies intertwining with the rustling of leaves as they pushed deeper into the treacherous terrain.

Luke led the way, his eyes scanning the surroundings for any sign of the hidden entrance. Each step they took brought them closer to their goal, but also closer to the hidden perils that lurked within this mysterious landscape. Pete walked close behind, his hand gripping a sturdy walking stick, ready to ward off any lurking dangers.

Violet and Madison followed suit, their gazes fixed on the muddy path ahead. A sense of anticipation mingled with the humid air, a shared understanding between them that they were embarking on a quest that would test their courage and resilience.

As they ventured deeper into the mangroves, the vegetation closed in around them like an intricate green tapestry. It seemed as if nature itself was conspiring to keep its secrets hidden from prying eyes. The undergrowth clawed at their legs, making each step difficult and cautious.

Nate's heart pounded in his chest, both from physical exertion and the thrill of the adventure. He couldn't help but wonder what lay in wait for them beyond these tangled roots and murky waters. The legends whispered in his ears, urging him to push forward, promising a reward worth their efforts.

Suddenly, Luke came to a halt, his eyes narrowing as he surveyed the area. "I think we're getting close," he said in a hushed voice. "According to the map, there should be a hidden entrance around here."

They gathered around him, Violet's eyes reflecting a mixture of excitement and nervousness. Madison offered a reassuring smile, her confidence unwavering despite the challenges they had faced thus far.

Luke stepped forward and knelt down, his fingers tracing the markings on the map. "The entrance should be concealed beneath these mangrove roots," he explained, pointing to a cluster of gnarled roots that seemed to form a natural archway.

With bated breath, they watched as Luke carefully peeled back the tangled roots, revealing a narrow opening leading into darkness. The air grew heavy with anticipation as they hesitated for a moment, contemplating the risks and rewards that awaited

41

them on the other side.

But their determination prevailed. Nate took the lead, his flashlight piercing through the veil of darkness that enveloped the underground cavern. As they descended into its depths, their footsteps echoed off the ancient stone walls, imbuing the space with a sense of reverence.

Suddenly, Madison's gasp broke the silence. They gathered around her, their flashlights illuminating the intricate hieroglyphics that adorned the walls. Nate's eyes widened in recognition as he deciphered fragments of the story embedded in these symbols—the story of Paradise Key's past and the necklace's elusive location.

The group moved as one, their hands tracing the contours of each carving, their minds racing with excitement and awe. The hieroglyphics spoke of ancient rituals and forgotten legends, each stroke hinting at the necklace's hidden whereabouts.

A surge of hope washed over them, their hearts lifting with renewed determination. They realized that they were one step closer to finding the lost diamond necklace and saving Paradise Key from its impending doom. The ancient hieroglyphics served as a beacon of guidance, leading them toward an uncertain yet promising future.

With eager anticipation, they continued deeper into the cavern, their footsteps echoing off the stone walls. The Legends of Paradise Key had unlocked another piece of the puzzle—an ancient secret that would bring them closer to their ultimate goal.

As they pressed forward, each step filled with purpose and resolve, they knew that time was running out faster than they had anticipated. The impending storm and the looming deadline for their community's demolition weighed heavily on their minds.

But in this moment, in the heart of the underground cavern, surrounded by the echoes of legends long past, they chose to focus on the present. They relied on their resourcefulness, their trust in each other, and the power of the legends that guided their every step.

Together, they ventured deeper into the depths of the cavern, their hearts aflame with hope and determination. The Legends of Paradise Key would stop at nothing to find the lost diamond necklace and protect their beloved community from the hands of destruction.

In the darkness of the hidden world beneath Paradise Key, they would find their answers—answers that would not only save their home but also uncover a legacy that had been waiting for them throughout the generations.

12

Trapped in Pursuit

The group ventured into an atmospheric old library, the creaking wooden floors greeting their every footstep. Dust particles danced in the air as they searched for answers hidden among the rows of dusty shelves. It was as if the scent of aged paper hung heavy in each breath they took, adding to the mystical ambiance that surrounded them.

Dr. Morgan, her eyes alight with determination, was drawn to a particular section filled with ancient texts. She ran her fingers along the spines, her touch reverent as she sought out the knowledge within those weathered pages. The weight of the past seemed to settle upon her shoulders as she chose books that held promises of untapped wisdom.

As the group gathered around a dimly lit table, the scraps of parchment and tattered books were carefully laid out before them. Nate's artistic talents came into play as he sketched symbols and landmarks that adorned the old texts, his hands dancing across the paper. Each stroke captured the essence of nature, evoking emotions that spoke to their souls.

"The answer lies within these riddles," Dr. Morgan said, her voice filled with a mix of excitement and reverence. "We must decipher their cryptic meanings to uncover the path leading to the necklace's location."

Madison leaned forward, her eyes scanning the pages before her. "Let's make sure we understand every clue before moving forward," she suggested, her voice tinged with determination.

Violet's fingers traced over the faded ink on one of the parchments, her eyes squinting as she tried to decipher its meaning. "This riddle references a hidden passage through stones marked with symbols," she exclaimed, pointing to a line that had caught her attention.

Pete scratched his beard thoughtfully, his mind working through possibilities. "These symbols may serve as a key to unlock our path," he mused aloud, his words carrying weight in the silence of the library.

Luke's gaze shifted from one riddle to another, his brows furrowed in concentration. "We can't afford to miss any details," he said, his voice steady and resolute. "Each word, each symbol must be analyzed with utmost care."

As they pieced together fragmented information and solved each riddle one by one, a sense of clarity began to emerge. They felt the weight of the past lifting, replaced by a renewed sense of purpose. With every revelation, their path became clearer, bringing them closer to finding the lost diamond necklace and protecting their community.

Hours passed as they delved deeper into the riddles, their minds consumed by a shared determination. Nate's creative insights became invaluable, as he drew connections between the symbols and the landmarks he had sketched earlier.

Finally, the last riddle was deciphered, leaving a hush over the group. The weight of their discoveries settled upon them, and they exchanged knowing glances that spoke volumes without words.

"The warehouse on the outskirts of Paradise Key," Luke declared, his voice filled with conviction as he pointed towards the final clue. "That's where our journey leads next."

Madison nodded, her eyes shining with unwavering resolve. "Let's prepare ourselves for what lies ahead," she said, her voice infused with anticipation.

With renewed determination and a newfound understanding of their own capabilities, the Legends of Paradise Key gathered their belongings and left the old library. The knowledge they had gained would guide them through treacherous terrain and uncharted paths, bringing them ever closer to unlocking the truth behind the legends and protecting their beloved community from destruction.

As they stepped back out into the world beyond those library walls, an air of confidence surrounded them. Their bond had grown stronger through adversity, and their hearts beat with a shared purpose that gave them strength in the face of uncertain futures.

Together, they embarked on the next leg of their journey, ready to face whatever challenges awaited them in the perilous trap-laden warehouse and beyond. The Legends of Paradise Key were prepared for whatever lay ahead, united in their quest to save their community and break free from the grip of greed and destruction.

13

Redemption's Path

The group reached an abandoned warehouse on the outskirts of Paradise Key, moonlight filtering through broken windows, casting eerie shadows on decaying crates and machinery. The air was thick with anticipation as they stepped cautiously into this treacherous environment, knowing that dangerous traps lay in wait to protect the mystical artifact.

Every step they took was filled with apprehension, their senses heightened as they scanned their surroundings for signs of danger. Madison's heart pounded in her chest, a mixture of excitement and fear coursing through her veins. She gripped Violet's arm tightly, seeking comfort in their shared bravery. Nate, his artist's intuition tingling, studied the decayed architecture, looking for clues that might guide them through the maze.

The atmosphere crackled with tension as they ventured further into the warehouse. It felt as if time stood still, each creak and groan of the aging structure echoing ominously in their ears. Luke's flashlight cast flickering shadows on the grimy walls, revealing graffiti tags and remnants of a forgotten time. Pete's keen eyes scanned every corner, searching for any hidden triggers that could activate the traps.

Suddenly, a low rumble filled the air as the ground beneath them began to tremble. The Legends of Paradise Key exchanged startled glances, realizing they had triggered a trap within the warehouse. Collapsing floors threatened to swallow them whole, swinging pendulums aimed to knock them off course. The room seemed alive with nefarious intentions, each obstacle designed to prevent anyone from reaching the hidden chamber rumored to house the lost diamond necklace.

Violet's nerves were tested as she expertly avoided a trap triggered by the slightest change in weight distribution. Every instinct screamed at her to freeze, but she pushed forward with unwavering determination. The trust she had earned from her friends fueled her courage and reinforced her belief in their ability to overcome any obstacle.

Adrenaline coursed through their veins as they pressed on, relying on their wits and teamwork to overcome each challenge. They communicated with subtle gestures and nods, their movements precise and calculated. Nate's artistic mind became a valuable asset as he deciphered symbols etched onto walls and determined safe paths to navigate through the hazardous terrain.

Each trap they successfully evaded brought them closer to their ultimate goal. The Legends of Paradise Key were resolute in their pursuit, their minds focused on the necklace's location and the fate of their community hanging in the balance.

Suddenly, an alarm blared, echoing through the abandoned warehouse. Panic set in as the group realized they had triggered an unforeseen security system. Flashing lights illuminated their surroundings, casting an ominous glow that made their hearts race even faster.

Luke's calm voice cut through the chaos. "Stay focused! We can't let this setback deter us," he urged, his eyes scanning for a way to disable the alarm and continue their desperate chase.

With quick thinking, Madison devised a plan. She used her knowledge of the surroundings to create a distraction, diverting the attention of the security system away from their location. The Legends of Paradise Key executed her plan flawlessly, slipping into the shadows unnoticed as they continued their relentless pursuit.

As they neared their final destination, the warehouse seemed to come alive with the ghosts of obstacles past. Collapsing floors threatened to swallow them whole, while swinging pendulums aimed to knock them off course. But with each challenge, their unity grew stronger.

The symbolism of their resilience served as a reminder of what they were fighting for. They weren't just unraveling a century-old legend or searching for a mystical artifact; they were protecting their home and preserving their heritage.

With one final trap looming ahead, their resourcefulness would be put to the ultimate test. They approached it cautiously, adrenaline coursing through their veins. The Legends of Paradise Key knew that failure wasn't an option — not when so much was at stake.

They took a deep breath and launched themselves into action, relying on every skill they had honed throughout their journey. Time seemed to stand still as they strained against the forces working against them.

And then... victory. With a collective sigh of relief, the group stood before the hidden chamber rumored to house the lost diamond necklace. Exhausted but elated, they marveled at how far they had come and what they had overcome.

For in this haunted warehouse filled with perilous traps, the Legends of Paradise Key had proven their resilience and determination. They were ready to face whatever challenges lay ahead, united by their shared purpose and their unwavering belief in the power of legends.

As they stepped into the chamber, a soft golden glow enveloped them, emanating from the forgotten artifact resting on its pedestal. The necklace's shimmering diamonds seemed to come alive, casting dancing reflections on the walls. It was a sight that took their breath away, reinforcing their conviction that this journey was more than a mere adventure.

In that moment, as they reached out to retrieve the necklace, they understood the true weight of their mission. Not only were they protectors of lore and history; they were guardians of Paradise Key's future. And with the mystical powers this necklace possessed, they knew they held the key to preserving their community and breaking free from the grip of greed and destruction.

With renewed determination burning in their eyes, the Legends of Paradise Key clasped hands around the necklace, forging an unbreakable bond that would guide them through the battles yet to come. As they left the warehouse behind, victory pulsated through their veins.

They had overcome treacherous trials and emerged stronger than ever. Their purpose burned brighter than any flame, urging them forward on their quest to save Paradise Key and become true legends in their own right.

14

United We Stand

The tension in Luke's living room was palpable, hanging heavy in the air as the group gathered for their crucial meeting. The fading sunlight cast long shadows across the worn wooden table, mirroring the uncertainty that clouded their hearts. Each member of the Legends of Paradise Key felt the weight of their community's future resting on their shoulders as they grappled with their conflicting emotions.

Luke, Pete, Nate, Violet, and Madison sat around the table, their faces etched with concern and determination. Conversation buzzed with an undercurrent of frustration and anxiety as they tried to find common ground amidst their differing viewpoints. Luke, driven by his passion and protective nature, argued fiercely for immediate action, determined to save their beloved Paradise Key at all costs.

Pete, ever the pragmatist, raised concerns about the risks involved in confronting powerful developers head-on. His voice quivered with a mix of fear for their safety and the desperation to protect his friends. Anxiety coiled within him as he grappled with the potential consequences of their actions.

Nate, a dreamer and artist at heart, envisioned a more creative approach. He proposed using their collective talents to raise awareness and rally support for their cause. His eyes glittered with hope, yearning for a peaceful resolution that would bring about lasting change.

Violet, bold and fearless, voiced her impatience and frustration. She pressed her fingertips against the table, leaning forward as she passionately argued for immediate action. Her unwavering determination to preserve their community fueled her words, each syllable emanating strength and resilience.

Madison, the intellect among them, listened intently to the different perspectives before offering her own insights. With a calm yet resolute voice, she advocated for a balanced strategy that reconciled their divergent views. She brought forth ideas rooted in research and analysis, urging them to consider both the short-term and long-term implications of their decisions.

The room crackled with tension as they debated, their voices rising and falling in a crescendo of conflicting opinions. Yet, beneath the surface, a deep sense of longing for unity emerged. They all shared a common love for their community and a desire to protect it from the encroachment of greed and destruction.

Realizing that their differences threatened to tear them apart, Luke called for a moment of silence. The room hushed as the Legends of Paradise Key looked at each other, truly seeing one another's hopes, fears, and unwavering commitment.

In this vulnerable moment, Luke spoke first. "We are all here because we deeply care about Paradise Key," he began, his voice steady and filled with sincerity. "We may have different ideas, but our love for our community unites us. We must find a way to channel our passion into a unified front."

A soft sigh escaped Pete's lips as he looked around the room at his friends. He recognized the strength in their bond, forged through countless adventures and shared experiences. "I may have been too focused on protecting everyone by avoiding risks," he admitted, regret coloring his words. "But I see now that it's not just about protecting ourselves—it's about fighting for what we believe in."

Nate's eyes sparkled with newfound understanding, his artistry paving the way for empathy. "We should channel our creativity into bringing people together," he suggested, a glimmer of hope dancing in his voice. "By inspiring others through our talents, we can amplify our message and rally support for our cause."

Violet nodded in agreement, her fiery spirit tempered by an appreciation for compromise. "Immediate action is important, but let's also consider the long-term impact of our choices," she offered, her tone measured yet resolute. "We need to strike a balance that ensures our community's survival while preserving its essence."

Madison, the voice of reason, smiled as she observed her friends' shifting perspectives. "Our individual strengths can complement each other," she suggested, her eyes shining with wisdom. "By combining our talents and finding common ground, we can create a strategy that is both bold and calculated."

As their voices tapered off, a renewed sense of unity settled among them. The realization dawned that they didn't have to choose between immediate action and cautious planning; they could marry the two approaches.

The Legends of Paradise Key understood that in order to overcome the challenges ahead, they had to embrace their differences and pool their individual strengths. Their shared love for their community would serve as the guiding force that propelled them forward.

With newfound resolve burning in their hearts, they clasped hands across the table. A quiet yet powerful bond was formed—one that would set the stage for their greatest challenge yet. As they prepared to face the battles ahead, their unity shone as a beacon of hope against the encroaching darkness threatening Paradise Key's very existence.

15

A Mysterious Guide

As the Legends of Paradise Key ventured deeper into the hidden cave, their footsteps echoed softly against the rocky walls. The air grew colder, and the scent of dampness permeated the surroundings. Every step heightened their anticipation, knowing that they were about to encounter a mysterious figure who held the key to their mission.

Their torches cast flickering shadows on the cavern walls, adding an eerie touch to the already mysterious atmosphere. Whispers seemed to echo through the darkness, hinting at an otherworldly presence waiting just ahead.

Suddenly, as they rounded a corner, a figure emerged from the shadows. It was Seraphina, the enigmatic guardian of Paradise Key. Her ethereal beauty took their breath away, her skin glowing softly like moonlit waves.

Seraphina's eyes sparkled with ancient wisdom and depth that seemed to reach into their very souls. They couldn't help but feel both humbled and awestruck in her presence. She radiated power, yet there was kindness and warmth in her gaze.

"Welcome, Legends of Paradise Key," Seraphina greeted them with a voice that resonated like a gentle breeze. "I have been expecting you."

Relief washed over the group as they listened intently to her words. They had come seeking answers, guidance, and perhaps even a touch of magic to aid them on their quest.

Seraphina spoke of the struggles Paradise Key had faced throughout its history—battles fought against greedy developers and the forces of nature. She recounted tales of legendary heroes who had risen in times of adversity, protecting their beloved community and preserving its heritage.

"Our ancestors faced challenges similar to the ones you face today," Seraphina said, her voice filled with a quiet strength. "They too were entrusted with the task of safeguarding Paradise Key. And now, it is your turn."

The weight of their mission settled upon them, mingling with a sense of honor and purpose. They had been chosen for this pivotal moment—to stand as guardians of their community's legacy and fight for its survival.

Seraphina's eyes swept over each member of the group, as if peering into their very souls. "You each possess qualities that make you uniquely suited to this task," she continued. "Luke, your passion and protective nature; Pete, your pragmatism and understanding of the bigger picture; Nate, your creativity and ability to inspire; Violet, your fearlessness and determination; Madison, your intellect and analytical mind."

Her words resonated deep within them, acknowledging their individual strengths while also emphasizing the importance of working together. It was a reminder that they could draw on each other's abilities to overcome the challenges ahead.

"But remember," Seraphina cautioned, her voice gentle but firm, "you are not alone in this journey. The spirit of Paradise Key stands with you, guiding your path. Trust in yourselves and the bonds you have forged as friends."

An energy seemed to envelop the group—subtle yet powerful. Their doubts and fears melted away, replaced by a steadfast resolve. Seraphina had reminded them that they were not just ordinary individuals; they were legends in the making.

With renewed determination burning in their hearts, the Legends of Paradise Key bid farewell to Seraphina, gratitude shining in their eyes. They stepped back into the darkness of the cave, united by a shared purpose and a newfound understanding of their role as guardians.

Armed with the knowledge imparted by Seraphina and fueled by their unbreakable bond, the group emerged from the cave with a renewed sense of purpose. They knew that their journey would not be easy, but they were prepared to face any challenges that lay ahead.

Together, they would protect their community's heritage, break free from the grip of greed and destruction, and ultimately write their own chapter in the legends of Paradise Key.

The weight of their mission settled heavily upon their shoulders, but they were ready to face whatever challenges awaited them. The path ahead would be treacherous, but their spirits were buoyed by the knowledge that they carried the legacy of Paradise Key within them. They walked with newfound determination, guided by the wisdom of Seraphina and fueled by their unbreakable bond.

The Legends of Paradise Key had been chosen for this task, and they would stop at nothing to protect their community from the forces that sought to destroy it. As they ventured further into the unknown, they knew that together, they could overcome any obstacle that crossed their path.

Their adventure had taken on a new dimension—a battle not just for a lost necklace, but for the preservation of their home and heritage. And armed with the strength bestowed upon them by Seraphina, they were ready to face whatever challenges lay ahead.

16

The Necklace's Hidden Potential

The Legends of Paradise Key stood on the secluded beach, bathed in the soft glow of the sunrise. The waves gently lapped against the shore, creating a soothing melody that accompanied their thoughts. Taking a moment to appreciate the beauty around them, they gathered in a circle, ready to explore the depths of their newfound connection with nature.

Nate closed his eyes and felt a surge of energy coursing through his body. Images began to form in his mind's eye—a vision of an ethereal Water Spirit. It shimmered like a clear stream, cascading gently down rocks before disappearing into the vast ocean. As Nate listened intently, he could almost hear the soothing sounds of water trickling in the background.

"The power of water flows through your veins," whispered the Water Spirit. "Use its fluidity to calm turbulent waves and extinguish destructive flames."

A profound understanding washed over Nate—through his

connection with the Water Spirit, he could manipulate water to protect Paradise Key. He felt a sense of responsibility and determination welling up inside him. With this newfound power, he knew he could counteract any destructive forces that threatened their cherished home.

Violet took her turn, feeling a gentle gust of wind caress her face as she connected with the Air Spirit. It appeared as an ethereal figure, its movements swift and graceful like a gentle breeze. The Air Spirit spoke with a voice that seemed to carry on the wind itself.

"The power of air is within you," the Air Spirit declared. "Harness its strength to clear obstacles and create pathways."

Violet nodded, her determination growing stronger with each passing moment. She understood that by calling upon the winds, she could open new paths for herself and her friends, guiding them safely through any challenges they might face.

Luke stepped forward, feeling a deep connection with the Earth Spirit. It appeared as a towering figure, rooted firmly to the ground. Its presence radiated stability and strength.

"The power of the earth runs through your veins," the Earth Spirit declared. "Draw upon its steadfast nature to anchor yourself and protect what is sacred."

Luke's understanding deepened as he embraced this newfound connection. With the earth's strength flowing within him, he knew that he could provide a solid foundation for his friends and defend Paradise Key against any threats.

Lastly, Pete approached, feeling a warmth radiating from within as he connected with the Fire Spirit. It appeared as a dancing flame, flickering with energy and intensity. Pete couldn't help but be drawn to its captivating allure.

"The power of fire burns in your soul," the Fire Spirit proclaimed. "Channel its energy to ignite passion, inspire others, and bring light into the darkest corners."

Pete nodded, fully aware of the responsibility that came with this newfound connection. He knew that by harnessing the power of fire wisely, he could motivate others to join their cause and bring hope to Paradise Key.

As they stood hand in hand on the beach, united by their shared bond and their newly discovered connections to the elemental forces of nature, tears glistened in their eyes. They had seen a future worth fighting for—a future where Paradise Key was saved and restored to its former glory.

With unity in their hearts and inspired by the powers bestowed upon them by the elemental spirits, the Legends of Paradise Key turned away from the beach, ready to face the challenges that awaited them. Guided by destiny and fueled by their newfound connections to nature, they embarked on their next steps—determined to turn their shared vision into a tangible reality.

In that moment, as they walked away, leaving footprints in

the sand, the sun rose higher in the sky. Its warm rays bathed Paradise Key in a golden glow—a silent testament to the power within their grasp. And as they ventured forth, they no longer saw themselves as mere individuals—they were a collective force, bound by their love for their home and their unwavering commitment to protect it.

The Legends of Paradise Key had been chosen for something greater than themselves. As they moved forward, the echoes of the elemental spirits resonated within them—a reminder of the power they now held and the destiny that awaited them.

17

Battle for Paradise Key

The Legends of Paradise Key stood at the entrance of the construction site, their eyes widening as they took in the devastation before them. The once vibrant and historic buildings now lay in ruins, reduced to piles of rubble and twisted metal. Dust hung heavily in the air, casting an eerie pall over the scene.

Luke's heart sank as he surveyed the destruction. This was supposed to be their home, a place filled with memories and community. Now, it had been marred by greed and disregard for the past. Determination fueled his every step as he stepped forward, his voice carrying a sense of authority.

"We can't let them continue," Luke said firmly. "We must do whatever it takes to stop them."

Nods of agreement rippled through the group as they locked eyes with each other. This battle was not just about preserving their own memories—it was about preserving the very essence of Paradise Key itself. They knew that if they didn't act now, they risked losing everything.

Pete's analytical mind kicked into action as he surveyed the surroundings. He noticed scattered debris and remnants of what was once homes and businesses. A plan formed in his mind—a way to stall the developers and buy themselves time to figure out how to use the necklace's powers against their adversaries.

"Look," Pete pointed towards the wreckage. "We can use these materials to create barriers and block their path."

Without hesitation, the friends sprang into action, moving large pieces of concrete and wood to strategic locations. They worked together seamlessly, their movements coordinated as if they had rehearsed this battle countless times.

As they constructed their makeshift barricades, each friend felt a renewed sense of purpose coursing through their veins. Their unity became palpable, a force stronger than any individual could muster alone. They were not just friends—they were protectors of something greater.

Luke's gaze swept over his friends, admiration and gratitude shining in his eyes. "We've come too far to give up now," he said, his voice steady. "Together, we can stand against greed and save Paradise Key."

The clash between the Legends of Paradise Key and the developers was fierce. Shouts and clashing of metal rang through the air as their opposing values collided. It was a battle between short-sighted gain and a deep-rooted love for their home.

Nate's artistic mind tapped into the powers of the necklace as he conjured a protective force field around himself. Glowing energy enveloped his body, shielding him from harm as he fought back against the relentless onslaught.

Violet, embodying her fearless nature, channeled the necklace's power to summon the forces of nature itself. Vines sprouted from the ground, twisting and entangling her adversaries, rendering them powerless against her determination.

Pete strategically maneuvered around the chaos, assessing the situation with a keen eye. He used his quick thinking to create diversions, causing confusion among their foes and buying precious seconds for his friends to regroup.

Luke stood at the forefront, his voice rallying their spirits. With each swing of his fists, he felt the necklace's power coursing through him—a surge of energy that fueled his every move. His unwavering resolve became a beacon of hope for his friends, inspiring them to fight on.

Through gritted teeth and determined gazes, the Legends of Paradise Key pressed forward. They pushed back against those who sought to destroy their community, defending what was sacred to them with every fiber of their beings.

As the battle raged on, victory seemed within reach. The developers' once-confident facade began to crumble under the sheer tenacity and resilience of the Legends. Their unified front proved too formidable to overcome.

Suddenly, like a ripple in a pond, Luke found himself face-to-face with Mr. Sullivan—the embodiment of greed and destruction. Their eyes locked, and for a moment, time stood still.

"I won't let you win," Luke declared, his voice brimming with defiance. "This is our home, and we will fight to the end to protect it."

Mr. Sullivan scoffed, a mix of arrogance and desperation in his gaze. "You may have a few tricks up your sleeve, but this land is mine. You can't stop progress."

Luke's resolve hardened as he took a step closer. "Progress shouldn't come at the expense of history and community," he said firmly. "We will never let you destroy what generations before us fought so hard to build."

With those words, Luke turned away from Mr. Sullivan, leaving him to stew in his own defeat. This battle was about more than just saving Paradise Key—it was about standing up for what was right and preserving the legacy of their beloved community.

As the dust settled and the defeated developers retreated, residents who had watched from a distance gathered around the Legends of Paradise Key. Applause filled the air, mingling with cheers of gratitude and relief.

The group embraced each other tightly, their tired but triumphant faces reflecting the satisfaction of a hard-fought battle won. Through unity and determination, they had repelled the forces of destruction and preserved their home.

In that moment of victory, the Legends of Paradise Key knew that they had not only saved a physical place but had also ignited a spark within their community—a spark that would continue to burn brightly, inspiring future generations to fight for what they believed in.

Their journey was far from over, but this battle had solidified their bond and fortified their resolve. With renewed strength and a shared purpose, they would continue to defend the legacy of Paradise Key—their home, their heritage, and their heart.

The Legends of Paradise Key emerged from the construction site, victorious but weary. They looked upon the landscape they had fought so hard to protect. Though the scars of battle were evident, they saw hope amid the ruins.

As they stood together, their hands clasped in a show of unity, the sun began to break through the clouds. Its warm rays bathed Paradise Key in a golden glow—a symbol of resilience and a promise of a brighter future.

"This battle is not over," Luke said, his voice filled with determination. "We've shown what we're capable of, and now we must keep fighting to preserve our home."

The Legends nodded in agreement, their faces etched with the understanding that their mission was far from complete. They would continue to defend Paradise Key against those who sought to exploit it for personal gain.

But as they looked at each other, there was a glimmer of something else in their eyes—hope. They had seen firsthand the power of friendship and community. They had witnessed the strength that could be unleashed when people stand together for a common purpose.

And armed with the necklace's powers and the unwavering belief that Paradise Key was worth fighting for, the Legends set off on their next chapter. They would face whatever challenges lay ahead with courage and determination, knowing that they were not alone.

The story of Paradise Key would not end in ruin. It would be a story of resilience, of triumph over adversity, and of the power of legends. The Legends themselves had become part of that story—protectors, guardians, and heroes.

With renewed purpose, they walked away from the battleground, ready to continue their fight. They would not let greed or destruction prevail. Together, they would ensure that Paradise Key's true potential would be revealed and cherished for generations to come.

For they were not just friends—they were the Legends of Paradise Key. And their legacy would endure long after the battle was won.

18

Community United: Rallying for Preservation

The sun shone brightly over Paradise Key Park, casting a golden hue on the gathered residents. Luke stood tall before the crowd, his voice projecting with an unwavering resolve and a passion that could not be ignored. Behind him, a makeshift stage adorned with banners and posters called for action to preserve their coastal neighborhood.

"I stand before you today not just as a resident of Paradise Key, but as a guardian of our heritage," Luke proclaimed, his eyes sweeping across the faces of his community. "We have seen the devastation that greed and disregard for our history can bring. But we refuse to let this happen to our beloved home."

The crowd listened intently, their curiosity mingling with a sense of urgency. Luke's words struck a chord deep within them. They had all experienced the beauty and magic of Paradise Key, and now they were being called to protect it.

"We have embarked on a journey, filled with challenges and triumphs," Luke continued. "But through it all, we have learned the power of unity and the strength of community. We may face towering obstacles, but together, we can overcome them."

As Luke spoke, memories of their shared experiences echoed in the hearts of the listeners. The group's adventures in unraveling the century-old legend of Paradise Key had touched each of their lives in profound ways. It was no longer just about saving their own memories—it was about safeguarding the soul of their community.

Violet stepped forward, her voice steady yet filled with emotion. "Paradise Key is more than just buildings and structures. It's where our dreams were born, where friendships were forged. We cannot let it be reduced to mere rubble."

Nate nodded in agreement, his artistic mind seeking the right words to convey their message. "Our story is intertwined with the very fabric of this place. Its preservation is not just our responsibility, but our duty to future generations."

Pete, with his analytical mind, took the stage next. "We have seen the power of the necklace, its mystical energy that connects us to the essence of Paradise Key. We must use this power to protect our home and create a legacy for all who come after us."

Luke's voice purred with gratitude as he looked out at his friends and community. "We are not alone in this fight," he declared. "In the face of adversity, we find strength and resilience within each other. Together, we can be a force that cannot be ignored."

72

The crowd erupted into applause, their cheers mingling with a renewed sense of determination. They had witnessed the Legends' unwavering commitment and bravery in facing down the developers. Now, they were ready to join the fight.

Paradise Key residents began exchanging ideas, discussing their role in preservation efforts. The energy of unity filled the air as they realized the potential of their collective voice. They knew that to preserve their beloved coastal neighborhood, they needed everyone on board.

As the community meeting came to an end, residents left with a newfound purpose in their hearts. They spread the word throughout Paradise Key, inspiring others to join their cause. Stories of Luke and his friends' adventures circulated, fueling a sense of urgency and a shared determination.

Through Luke's impassioned speech, the residents of Paradise Key had been stirred from apathy to action. They now understood their collective responsibility to protect their shared heritage and ensure that future generations would experience the beauty and magic that had enchanted them for so long.

The journey had begun—Paradise Key would not be lost without a fight. And by standing together as a united community, they would be unstoppable.

19

The Legacy of Heroes

The sun had set completely, leaving behind a canvas of twinkling stars in the velvety night sky. Luke, Violet, Nate, Pete, and Madison found themselves on the beach, their feet sinking into the cool sand as gentle waves lapped at the shoreline. There was an air of tranquility and contentment, a sense that everything had fallen into place.

Luke looked around at his friends, taking in their smiling faces illuminated by the soft glow of starlight. The celebration in town could wait—for now, this quiet moment belonged to them alone. They stood together in a tight circle, their arms linked as a testament to their unwavering bond.

"It's hard to believe how far we've come," Violet said, her voice filled with emotion. "From the moment we started unraveling the secrets of the legend to this very moment, it's been an incredible journey."

Nate nodded in agreement, his eyes reflecting the starlight.

"Our story has become intertwined with Paradise Key itself," he mused. "Our determination and bravery will forever be a part of this place."

Pete, ever the analytical thinker, chimed in with a thoughtful expression. "Through our journey, we have discovered the power of unity and community," he said. "We showed everyone that together, we can overcome any obstacle."

Their words hung in the air, mingling with the gentle caress of the ocean breeze. Luke smiled, his heart filled with gratitude for his friends. "You are all true legends," he said. "Legends who have protected our home and inspired others to do the same."

As they stood there, their footprints creating patterns in the sand behind them, they felt a surge of pride and accomplishment. They had faced towering obstacles and outsmarted greedy developers. They had connected with the history and soul of Paradise Key. And most importantly, they had rallied a community to fight for what they believed in.

"There's no denying that our journey has forever changed us," Madison said, her voice filled with newfound confidence. "We've grown, not just individually, but as a team. We've become stronger and more resilient."

Violet reached out to squeeze Madison's hand, a silent expression of support and love. The necklace, its mystical energy protected and preserved, hung around Violet's neck as a symbol of their unity and strength.

As they gazed out at the vast expanse of the ocean, a sense of serenity settled over them. They were no longer just friends; they were bound by an unbreakable bond forged through shared triumphs and challenges.

With a renewed sense of purpose, Luke turned his attention back to his friends. "Our journey doesn't end here," he said. "There is still work to be done. We must continue to protect and preserve Paradise Key, not just for ourselves, but for future generations."

Nate nodded, his eyes shining with determination. "By standing together, we can ensure that the magic and beauty of this place endure."

Pete's analytical mind kicked into gear, already envisioning a plan for the next steps. "We must rally the community once again," he said. "Share our story, inspire others to join the cause. Together, we can create a legacy that will last."

The friends exchanged knowing glances, the weight of their responsibility settling on their shoulders. But there was no doubt in their minds—they were ready for whatever challenges lay ahead.

They turned away from the beach, their footprints slowly being washed away by the tide. As they made their way toward town, they could hear the distant sound of celebration growing louder.

It was time to join their community, to revel in their victory and share stories of triumph. But in their hearts, they knew that this was just the beginning.

Their legends would live on, forever etched in the history of Paradise Key. And as long as they stood together, united in purpose and friendship, there was nothing that could stand in their way.

With a final glance at the starlit beach behind them, they walked hand in hand along the moonlit path, their determination and love guiding them forward.

The journey was far from over, but they were ready to face whatever came their way.

Together, the Legends would protect Paradise Key and ensure that its magic and beauty endured for generations to come.

About the Author

Tate was born Timothy Sean, in Saint Petersburg, FL. in 1974, living there with one older sister and a loving family. Tim enjoyed youth baseball and football into high school at Gibbs, graduating from the Pinellas County Center for the Arts (PCCA) and moving to Pittsburgh in 1992, to attend the acting conservatory at Carnegie-Mellon University. At PCCA and CMU, Tim was trained under world renowned faculty in the theater arts. Research, development and creation of a character; leading into show specific performance choices, scene work, Black box theatrical performances and finally, large auditorium sized venues filled with hundreds or thousands of audience members, all packed in together, their energy palpable on stage the moment you enter. Tim spent the summer of 1994 living in the United Kingdom, First, residing in London's Piccadilly Circus district. Then, Tim moved up to Balliol College in Oxford, studying Shakespeare and classical writing. Later, Tim met his father, who had traveled over from the US, and the two travelled the southern half of Ireland together, the McGhees home country. The McGhees spent a significant portion of the week on the western coast. This included a stay in Galway and an overnight trip on Inishmaan (one of the Aran Islands) where Tim hiked with his dad to find one of his favorite writers, John Millington Syne's chair, to pray.

Back in America, Tim went on to act in leading and character roles in main stage and network productions for PCCA, Carnegie-Mellon University and after graduation with honors in May of 1996, after a brief residency in the West Greenwich Village neighborhood of New York City, Tim moved to Los Angeles in the fall of 1996, after signing with the Cosden Talent Agency in Hollywood. In 1997, Tim guest starred on NBC's Saved by the Bell, CW's Sweet Valley High, and then received the SAG guest starring role, on USA's Pacific Blue, where Tim took the SAG union name, Tate, Living off the Sunset Strip in West Hollywood, working in film, commercials and television for 6 years, Tate continued creating and writing his own poetry and short stories, as part of the artistic training he had received from his earlier days attending PCCA "Exhibit X." and CMU. Tate entered and performed his one man show "The Savage Window,' written in college, for the National Poetry Conference held in Anaheim, CA. in 1999. Tate continued acting under the new direction of a personal manager, also writing two feature screenplays: AMEN and SILVERGIRL, during that time; until the fall of 2001, when Tate was offered an opportunity to return to graduate school and work towards a master's degree in applied behavior analysis from the Florida Insititute of Technology (FIT.)

Back in Florida in 2002, Tate committed to the new career in Behavior Analysis, working with those in need back in St. Petersburg, FL. In 2010, Tate and his wife got married on the beach. Tate and his wife welcomed their first child, a son, in 2012. In 2014, Tate welcomed the birth of their new daughter. Meanwhile in 2014, Tate was also invited to Bosnia and Herzegovina to present of a special assignment as a Behavior Analyst. Tate took residence in Paris for the month of November of 2017, writing from the Saint Michel neighborhood, witnessing the beauty of the Notre Dame cathedral only months before the destructive inferno. In 2019, Tate continued writing, leading to the episodic series THIS MOMENT IN TIME, now available on Kindle Vella and later the feature screenplay GANGPLANK. In 2023, Tate is currently practicing ABA now over 20 years and continuing to develop several other projects. Tate enjoys service, spending time with his family, writing, movies and music, following/attending sports games, concerts, surfing, Today, Tate thanks Jesus Christ above all else and looks to be a loving husband, father, friend to all, practicing BCBA and author with participation across many genres. THANK YOU FOR YOUR INTEREST.

Also by Tate McGhee

King of the Night

A young boy named Miles discovers courage, knowledge & bravery in the dark of the night after he meets a cat named Shadow. Together they travel a mythical journey far and wide overcoming fear while unlocking the beauty of imagination.

The Gangplank: Heist in a Hurricane

As Category 4 hurricane "Hector" barrels down on Tampa Bay, five courageous children embark on a perilous treasure hunt on Halloween night 2032, to save their neighborhood from disappearing into the Gulf under storm surge. Faced with their sinking city, they defy local rumors and venture into the underground tunnels below their Jungle Prada neighborhood, racing against time and facing dangerous obstacles, they must find a stolen diamond necklace rumored to be hidden deep within the tunnels, whose value has the financial potential to save a neighborhood. With history, mystery, and friendship as their guides, these brave children uncover a century-old legend and ultimately save their community from disappearing into the Gulf.

Click: Ending School Shootings Using Applied Behavior Analysis

In the aftermath of his father's tragic death in a school shooting, a brilliant graduate student specializing in Applied Behavior Analysis (ABA) embarks on a groundbreaking journey. Using his thesis defense as a platform, he presents an innovative plan to prevent future acts of violence by addressing each of the 7 dimensions of ABA. What sets this book apart is the incorporation of cutting-edge technology, such as AI and virtual reality, to provide real-life illustrations and simulations. Readers will engage with the main character's personal journey and witness their determination to make a positive impact. Explore a thought-provoking topic, learn about ABA, and discover practical strategies for reducing or eliminating school shootings in this gripping blend of fiction and reality.

Mastering Behavior Change

Prepare to embark on a transformative journey towards personal growth and lasting behavior change with "Mastering the Science of Behavior Change" by Tate McGhee, MS, BCBA. This exceptional novel defies conventions by presenting the complex concepts of applied behavior analysis in an easily digestible format suitable for all ages. Mastering Behavior Change follows Jacob Thompson, Ethan Sullivan, and Oliver Reed as they bond over similar views on what brought them to their annual state conference and Applied Behavior Analysis. Readers will gain unique insight on how to apply behavior analysis techniques to effect enduring changes in their own lives. With its seamless integration from theory to practice and back, this remarkable guide empowers readers to take control of their behavior more effectively while paving the way towards lasting personal growth.

This Moment in Time

This Moment in Time follows a group of former college friends as they come together for their 25-year class reunion and grapple with unresolved love from their past. Set against the backdrop of Carnegie-Mellon University in the early nineties, the story delves into the lives of these characters, exploring the challenges they face in midlife, such as parenting, care giving, and financial struggles. The book takes readers on an emotional roller coaster, shifting between present-day events and memories from their college years. It emphasizes the power of imagination and creativity, reminding readers that their voices matter and that the world needs their unique contributions. With its relatable characters and thought-provoking themes, This Moment in Time is a captivating read that will leave readers inspired to embrace their own creativity and find meaning in their lives.

www.ingramcontent.com/pod-product-compliance
Lightning Source LLC
Chambersburg PA
CBHW070642130626
46555CB00006B/2662